The Girl with the
Sunshine
Smile

Karen McCombie

With illustrations by
Cathy Brett

Barrington Stoke

*For Gözde, who always has a
sunshine smile*

First published in 2020 in Great Britain by
Barrington Stoke Ltd
18 Walker Street, Edinburgh, EH3 7LP

www.barringtonstoke.co.uk

This 4u2read edition based on *The Girl with the
Sunshine Smile* (Barrington Stoke, 2014)

Text © 2020 Karen McCombie
Illustrations © 2014 & 2020 Cathy Brett

The moral right of Karen McCombie and Cathy Brett to be
identified as the author and illustrator of this work has been
asserted in accordance with the Copyright, Designs and
Patents Act, 1988

A CIP catalogue record for this book is available
from the British Library upon request

ISBN: 978-1-78112-923-4

Printed in China by Leo

The Girl with the

Sunshine Smile

Th
be
dat , a

Contents

Chapter 1
Bad to Be Good?

I have a secret.

A secret *talent*.

I don't ever speak about it – well, only to my best friend Bex.

If I told anyone else, I'd sound like I was a total show-off. I'd sound like I was all, "Look at me! Look at me!"

That's because my talent is looking ... nice.

What I mean is, I'm good at looking pretty in photos. *And* I'm good at smiling.

See?

That makes me sound bad, doesn't it?

But my nice smile – and the fact that I look pretty in photos – is really important to my family. My family of me and Mum.

Mum's special talent is sewing. When my dad left, she set up her own business making dresses for bridesmaids and flower girls. Work was slow at first but that changed when Mum got a stall at a wedding fair. She had to take me with her and I played while grown-ups wandered around and looked at fancy things they could buy for their Big Days.

While we were at the fair, a woman at the next stall gave Mum some advice.

1. Get a website.

2. Post photos of a cute child on it, modelling the dresses.

3. Use *me* as the model, cos of what the woman called my "sunshine smile"!

Mum took the woman's advice.

She dressed me up, put flowers in my hair, a posy in my hands and – *snap!* – took my picture.

I was nearly three then and I'm twelve now, and I *still* model for her. At weekends, we go to lots of wedding fairs in posh hotels, where they call me "the girl with the sunshine smile".

Chapter 2
Will They, Won't They?

We're at one of those posh hotels today and a woman has stopped at our stall.

She stares at my dress in a totally dreamy way.

"Ooo ..." she murmurs.

The dress is made of white linen and has a buttercup-yellow sash around the waist.

"Here, take a leaflet," Mum says, but the woman is lost in wedding daydreams.

"Thanks," the man with her says. He grins at Mum and looks at the front of the leaflet. "*The Sunshine Dress Company*," he reads out loud. "Do you do any in my size?"

That's pretty funny and Mum giggles. It's not just funny cos he's a man. It's cos he's a

very *messy* man. Most of the boyfriends here at the wedding fair are clean and tidy. They have combed their hair and shaved. They're wearing nice shirts and smart jeans.

This man has messy stubble, dark red hair that sticks up at all angles and jeans that are covered in dirt.

"Hey, Danny – can you see my little flower girl Alice in this?" the woman says at last.

"Yep," the man says. "She'd look very nice. Not like my boys, who'll just want to wear their skate shorts."

"They will not!" the woman says. She gives the man a jokey slap on the arm but she seems a bit cross.

"Your boys aren't keen on getting smart, then?" Mum asks.

"Danny's son Charlie said he'll only come to the wedding if he can bring his skateboard," the woman says. She rolls her eyes.

"My youngest son, Leo, told me he'll only come if I promise to buy him a pet rat," the man adds. "But I think his brother Frank put him up to that."

"You have *three* sons?" Mum says. "Wow, your house must be noisy!"

I'm thinking the same thing. Me and Mum live in a small flat in a block by the park. I love our peaceful, girly home. I can't imagine living with three roaring, loud boys.

"Ha!" the woman snorts. "Danny has *four* sons."

"Four sons, a cat with three legs and a bike-repair business," Danny says. He points to the dirt on his jeans. "Don't forget about that."

"How could I forget?" the woman says. "And how could you forget that you promised to come with me today?"

Now *she's* pointing at the man's dirty clothes. Seems like he didn't have time to change out of them.

"Aw, come on, Jen! I said sorry, didn't I?" he says. "Let me buy you a coffee and cake to make up for it ..."

As they go off towards the cafe, the man gives me and Mum a wave and a smile.

Chapter 3
Next, Please!

A few weeks after the wedding fair, I'm back at school and there's a note stuck to the gym door. "Line up here for School Photos," it says.

The gym windows light up from the camera flashes inside.

"I *hate* getting my photo taken!" Bex moans as we wait in a long line. She checks her braces and her messy dark curls in a tiny mirror.

"It's OK," I say. I'm happy that we're out in the fresh air instead of stuck in the classroom.

"It's OK for you, Meg!" Bex says, and she passes me the mirror. "You've had your photo taken a gazillion times."

She's right. It's not just Mum who has taken my photo over the years. My picture's been in the local newspaper and even a couple of wedding magazines. The line for school

photos seems to be taking ages and, as I wait, I think about how it's been fun modelling Mum's dresses over the years. I should make the most of it while I still can.

"Hey, Meg, I'm talking to you," Bex says. "Are you OK? You've been lost in your own little world a lot, the last while."

"Have I?" I gaze up from the mirror and frown at Bex. But there's no time to think about what she's just said, because the line of students moves forward.

At last we're in the gym and Bex is in front of the photographer.

"Smile!" he tells her. "Come on – you can do better than that!"

Bex pushes her curls from her face, gives a quick, shy grin and the flash pops.

"Next!"

My turn.

I slide onto the stool. I look up and smile my best smile but the photographer's not looking at me.

"Sorry – be with you in a sec," he mutters as he fiddles with his camera.

That spare second lets me mull over what Bex said.

I suppose I have been less chatty over the last few weeks. Less sunshiny too – at least inside. It's because of Mum, I realise. We have always been close. But the last few weeks, something has been different – it feels like there's a distance between us …

The photographer interrupts my thoughts. "OK, let's have a big smile," he calls out.

FLASH!

In that moment it hits me – Mum is hiding something from me, isn't she?

And – oops – I think I just forgot how to smile.

Chapter 4

I Spy

I am spying on my own mother.

So is my friend Bex.

Together we will find out what it is that Mum is hiding from me.

Bex lives two floors above me in our block of flats and tonight I'm having a sleepover at hers. We're at the bedroom window, peering at the road below.

"Where did she say she was going?" Bex asks as she passes me a packet of cookies.

"Book club," I tell her. "Again."

I'm no detective but it just doesn't add up. I haven't seen any new books in our flat. And I'm pretty sure most book clubs only meet once a month. Mum has been going out every Saturday for weeks now.

"Look – there's your mum!" Bex says.

Yep, it's Mum, wearing her favourite deep purple dress and cool ankle boots.

Bex and I look at each other – we're both thinking the same thing. My mum doesn't look like she's going to a book club. And then Bex says, "Hey, who's *that*?"

We both watch as Mum waves to a man on the other side of the street. He waves back, then he crosses the road. He puts his arm round Mum and they stroll off together.

I stare at them in shock. "I don't know," I tell Bex.

But then I notice the man's dark red hair and all of a sudden I remember ...

He's the man with the dirt on his jeans and the cross girlfriend. From the wedding fair.

Mum is dating *him* ...? Mum is dating someone else's husband-to-be. How could she? How dare she?

*

"Hello, darling!" Mum says as I walk back into our flat the next morning. She's at her sewing machine. "Did you have fun at Bex's?"

I ignore her. It's no good acting as if everything is OK. How can everything be OK when my own mother has a secret boyfriend?

Someone else's boyfriend!

"Do you want to tell me what's going on?" I ask.

"What do you mean, Meg?" Mum says.

"Please don't pretend you're in a book club," I say, and I pull my best "don't-lie-to-me" face. "Danny – that's his name, isn't it?" I ask.

Mum gasps. "It's not what you think," she blurts out.

I go silent. I'm not going to make this easy for her. Not when she's been keeping secrets. *Bad* secrets.

"Danny phoned me about a week after that wedding fair and asked me out," she says. "I was surprised – till he explained. Jen, the woman he was with that day, she's his sister, not his girlfriend."

It takes a minute for the truth to sink in.

"OK," I say at last, in a hurt voice. "But why have you kept this hidden from me?"

"Oh, Meg," Mum says. "We had to be sure how we felt about each other," she tells me. "Before I told you it was for real, I mean."

For real. *That* sounds serious.

"In fact, I was going to tell you today," Mum carries on, "because Danny has invited us for tea. Is that OK?"

Mum bites her lip and waits for me to speak.

She wants me to say yes. She wants a sunshine smile.

But I'm not in the mood. Anyway, what is there to smile about? It's always been just me and Mum – best friends as well as mother and daughter. But all of a sudden, everything has changed. Big time.

Chapter 5

What a Welcome (not)

Four boys stare at me. One is a teenager, one is a little kid and two are in between. The littlest one is picking his nose.

I feel sick.

Not because of nerves or the nose-picking. (Gross!) I feel sick because Danny and his four staring sons live on a boat.

OK, a barge.

Their home is a giant hunk of wood floating on the river. It's called the *Bluebell* and is surrounded by lots more boats and barges. And standing here on the open top deck is making me feel like I'm about to vomit.

"Well, who is going to give Meg a tour of the *Bluebell*?" Danny asks his sons in a too-happy voice.

"Not me!" a boy with dark hair yells. I've been told this is Frank. He's eight.

"Not me too!" yells another boy – four-year-old Leo.

Then they both run off sniggering.

"What about you?" Danny says to a tall, lanky boy. He must be Charlie. He is fourteen, the oldest of Danny's sons.

"Got to take this call!" Charlie says – even though his mobile hasn't even rung.

"Well, Seb – that leaves you," Danny says. He nods at the last boy, who is twelve, same as me.

"Ughhh," Seb sighs, and he rubs a hand through his mop of hair. "Do I *have* to?"

"Seb!" his dad says with a shocked laugh.

"OK, OK," Seb grumbles. He waves at me to follow him down an open hatch.

"Go on, Meg," Mum says. "This place is so amazing! You'll love it!"

"I don't think I will," I mutter to myself as I take careful steps backwards down the ladder.

"So you just saw the deck, where we eat if
the weather is OK, and where Dad works," Seb
says. He sounds bored. "And this ... this is the
living room and the kitchen."

As my feet touch the floor, I turn and look. The barge inside reminds me of a caravan. Bench-style seats line the walls. There is a built-in cupboard with a tiny telly stuck on top. Tatty, short curtains hang on droopy wires at the windows.

This place would look cute if it was tidy, which it's not.

I have never seen so much boy mess. Trainers, jumpers, bags are everywhere. I kick away a grungy stray sock with the toe of my ballet pump. (Yuck.)

"Dad's bedroom is through the back," Seb says. He doesn't even bother to look at me. "Ours are on the bottom level."

"Is that where your bathroom is too?" I ask. I feel woozy again.

"Uh-huh," Seb mutters, and he nods to another hatch.

"I can manage," I tell him as I hurry over to the top of a set of steep steps. I don't need his company for this – especially if I really am going to be sick.

In the bathroom, I splash cold water on my face in the weeny sink. I feel better instantly. And, while I'm here, I decide I'll try to have a wee. There's no lock on the bathroom door, so I shove the washing basket against it to keep it closed.

I sit down on the loo and think of what Mum told me this morning – that Danny and his sons moved to the barge after the boys' mum died. Leo was only a baby back then and Danny had to work part-time so he would be able to look after him. So he sold their normal house and bought this barge, which was much cheaper.

"Danny knew it was right when he saw the boat's name," Mum said on the way here. "Bluebells were his wife's favourite flower ..."

It's a really sweet, sad story.

THUD!

Uh-oh.

The door swings open. The washing basket spills socks and pants like dirty cloth confetti

all over the floor. Frank is standing there, staring at me.

Me with my jeans around my ankles ...

"Ha ha ha ha ha!" he yelps, then runs away.

He's going to tell his brothers about this, isn't he?

And I'm going to tell Mum that I'm never, ever visiting the *Bluebell* again, no matter how sad and sweet Danny's story is.

Chapter 6

Please, No!

The next Sunday, we're at another wedding fair. I'm trying to look happy for the sake of all the couples who are strolling past Mum's stall but it's not working. After the total *shame* of what happened on the barge, I have lost my sunshine smile.

I glance around for Mum but I see she's still outside. She's trying to phone our landlord, cos there's been a bit of a disaster at home.

While Mum is busy, I sneak a call of my own. It isn't very classy to use a mobile when

you're modelling a pretty bridesmaid's dress
but I need to speak to Bex.

"Hey, you!" I say as soon as she picks up.

"Hey, you!" she says back. "Feeling better?"

She means the loo disaster of course. I will never feel better about that.

"Worse!" I tell her. "We had a flood in our flat today. A pipe burst – and the plumber has no idea why!"

"Really?" Bex gasps. "That sounds bad, Meg!"

"It is. The place is a *mess*. I hope it's easy to fix, cos Mum cracked a joke just now that made me feel ill."

"Yeah?" Bex says. "What was that?"

"She said that if the flat needs lots of work, then maybe we'll have to go and stay on Danny's barge."

"Ha!" Bex snorts.

"Can you imagine?" I say. "Me on that barge. With all those *boys*!"

Then I spot Mum coming back to the stall.

"Got to go, Bex," I say. I switch my mobile off and hide it behind my back.

I'm feeling giggly after talking to my best friend. But that feeling fades pretty fast when I see Mum's face.

She looks hassled. Like she has news she doesn't want to tell me. Bad news.

Please, no ... *not* the barge!

Chapter 7
Moving-in Day

Most people don't take sea-sickness pills when they move house, do they?

But I've taken one. The rocking of Danny's barge really gets to me. And I reckon I'll have to take one every day that we're staying here. Mum says that's going to be at least one week. Maybe two, until the broken pipe in our flat is fixed.

It's just my luck. My *bad* luck, I mean.

I tried hard not to come here today. I don't want to be on this scruffy, crowded, always-moving barge. I begged Bex to let me stay at hers but there's no room.

So here I am, standing in the cabin that is mine for now.

It's small as a wardrobe and smells of dust and damp. There's a tiny bed and a bare rail to hang my clothes on, and that's it – apart from a mirror that hangs lop-sided on the wall.

My face in the lop-sided mirror looks like thunder. How am I going to survive this week? Maybe I'll just lock myself away in this tiny room. Stay away from those boys and—

"Aaaaarghh!!"

I can't help yelping, as something has just jumped in the open porthole window.

I see a blur of fur. It's Tigger – Danny and the boys' three-legged cat!

Just as I get over that fright, I scream again
when a low-down panel in the wall moves and
something else bursts into my room. Hold on …

It's two somethings. Frank and Leo!

Now I remember what else Mum told me.
On the barge, all the rooms connect like this, to
make escape hatches in case of a fire.

"Boo!" the boys yell. "Ha ha ha!"

I've only been here five minutes and already it's a nightmare.

Get me out of here!

Chapter 8

The Worst Photo Ever

I have stayed on the barge for three long days now.

It's been hard.

The barge tilts at low tide, so the water in the bath runs to one end. When I tried to use my new hairdryer, all the lights went out, as the barge has a weak power supply.

I have hidden away in my cabin a lot – doing my homework, reading, listening to music. (My wheelie case is wedged against the escape-hatch door.)

Bex has been brilliant. Today she took me back to her place for a real treat – a non-squint bath in a boy-free flat. It was total luxury. I lay there for ages and listened to the playlist blasting out from her room. (Bex chose all my favourite tracks.) And, after my bath, I spent a long, long, *long* time blow-drying my hair without the power going off.

Bex's mum asked me to stay for tea but – get this – my mum said no!

When I called her, she told me I had to come back to the barge. She and Danny had made something special for tea.

Whoop-dee-doo!

It could be a fancy meal fit for royalty but I'd rather share a bowl of crunchies with Tigger the three-legged cat than sit and eat with Danny's four annoying sons.

I sigh and stomp along the gangway, then stop dead.

The *Bluebell* is *twinkling*.

Ropes of soft white fairy lights are strung back and forth above the deck. I know those fairy lights – Mum sells them on her stall for weddings. It's kind of funny to see them here on this scuzzy boat. They make it seem almost magical.

"Mum?" I call out as I clamber on board.

"Do you like it, Meg?" she asks. She sounds shy and hopeful.

"It looks good," I say. "Pretty." Then I notice an odd thing. My heart lurches a bit – it feels like the boat rocking in the river. Leo is holding Mum's hand. I'm not sure how that makes me feel.

"Hey, Meg!" Danny calls. "Can you take this?"

His head is peeking out from the hatch on deck and he's holding a tray of food.

"Sure," I reply.

I drop my schoolbag on the deck and it flops to one side. Some of my stuff tumbles out but I'll sort it in a sec – I need to help Danny.

"Wow," I say when I put the tray down on the table. There's tons of food and it all looks great.

"Daddy's been cooking all day," Leo says. "And I put the flowers in the vase!"

I smile at the clump of dandelions in a jam jar.

I feel myself relax here for the very first time. Maybe a few more days on the *Bluebell* won't hurt, after all.

"Ha ha ha ha!"

That sounds like Frank.

"Nice picture – not!" Seb cackles.

I spin around and see what has fallen out of my bag to be snatched up by the boys. "Give me that!" I snap.

It's my school photo – the one that was taken when I realised Mum had a secret she was keeping from me. It's the worst photo of me *ever*. My mouth is hanging open and I look stunned, like I've had an electric shock.

I grab the photo from Seb and chuck it over the side of the barge. I hope it sinks to the bottom of the river.

If only I could do the same to Seb and Frank.

I wish.

Chapter 9
So Cool?

It's Friday and it's movie night. Not at the local cinema but on the deck of a barge which belongs to one of Danny's neighbours.

A screen on a stand flaps gently in the breeze. Little kids are kicking cushions into wiggly rows for people to sit on once the sun sets and the film starts. Some teenagers are handing out popcorn in mugs.

"Popcorn?" Bex asks me.

"No thanks," I say to Bex, who is here to keep me company. And to listen to my moans.

(I've just found out that we have to stay *another* week.)

"Watching a film outdoors on a river ..." Bex murmurs. "It's so cool, Meg!"

Cool? I don't think so. It's mad!

"So where are Danny's sons?" Bex asks. She twirls a curl in her fingers and gazes around at all the boys and girls – some on the deck, some on the river bank – who are chatting, laughing and fooling around.

"The tall boy over there is Charlie," I say. Charlie's one of the popcorn waiters, handing out mugs. "And that one is Seb." Seb is helping his dad move a table.

"Oh, *he's* cute!" Bex says.

No! I don't want her to think that! What next? Will she say that Frank and Leo are adorable? Who knows where they are but—

"RAARGGGHHH!"

The loud roar makes me jump and the thud on my back takes me by surprise.

I slip to one side, my balance gone. I lurch and stumble and reach for Bex but I miss her and clutch at thin air instead.

Then all of a sudden I tip over the handrail.

A whoosh of air.

A yell for help.

Then the cold water takes my breath away.

Chapter 10

The Opposite of OK

I'm in water again but at least this time it's hot. And bubbly.

"Meg?" Mum calls from the other side of the bathroom door. "Are you OK?"

How can I be OK? I fell into a river. All because Frank was showing Leo some so-called "deadly ninja moves" and the little weasel crashed into me.

"Meg?" Mum calls again. "Can I come in?"

Of course she can come in. There's no lock on the stupid door of this stupid bathroom on this stupid boat.

I don't reply but Mum comes in anyway and sits on the edge of the bath.

"Frank really is *very* sorry," she says, and strokes my hair. (It still smells of muddy water, even after I've shampooed it twice.)

I shrug. All I can think of is how scary it was in the water. I'll never forget that feeling of going under. When I got to the surface, I spluttered for breath and grabbed the life ring that Charlie threw to me. And then Danny and Seb pulled me up to safety, with all those faces staring. Oh, the *shame* ...

"He's made this for you," Mum says.

She holds out a piece of paper folded in half. It says "SORRY!" in big letters, in all different colours. She opens it for me. "And Leo drew this."

Inside is a wonky picture of something that looks like a fish in a wig.

"It's you, Meg," Mum says with a little smile. "As a mermaid!"

Mum may be smiling but I'm not.

It doesn't matter how cute the boys are. The "sorry" card and the fish-in-a-wig drawing won't make me change my mind.

I can't stand it here and I am *not* staying.

Chapter 11

Hard to Be Happy

I'm not in the mood to be wearing this bridesmaid's dress.

"Meg, you're frowning again," Mum teases me. "You'll scare my customers away. Stop it!"

Well, that's easy for her to say but it's hard to be happy.

Smiling couples are all around me at today's wedding fair. They don't have a clue that last night I got dunked in a river. That my mum got upset when I told her I was leaving. That I slept at my best friend's house.

"Look, I'm going to phone the landlord again," Mum says. "We'll see if we can get back to the flat any sooner. OK?"

I give her a "yes please" nod. At least she's trying to make things better. I really hope we can move back in – I have a sore neck from sleeping on Bex's hard bedroom floor.

Mum drifts away to make her call ... and I realise someone is talking to me.

"Excuse me – hello?" It's a little kid, tugging at my dress. That's not good – I can't get dirty fingerprints on this! I go to tug it free and then I see that the little kid is Leo.

"Meg, *please* don't be angry with us!" he says, and he holds out a tatty bunch of dandelions.

I feel the frown fall from my face. It's the cutest thing ever.

"Thank you, Leo," I say. I take the dandelions and sniff them as if they smell lovely and not like cat wee.

"We're all really sorry," I hear a man's voice say. "Please can we start again?"

I look up and see Danny, with Charlie, Seb and Frank. The three bigger boys look shy and sorry instead of sneery.

I try to smile but I think I've forgotten how to.

Is it too late?

For me to get the sunshine back in my smile *and* for us all to get along?

Chapter 12

One Year Later

The twinkling ropes of fairy lights sway in the evening breeze.

The blue sky is streaked pink and peach as the sun sets. It's warm and the crowd of people on the top deck of Danny's barge are in a party mood.

I'm watching it all from a chair tucked in the prow of the boat.

"Your mum looks so lovely!" Bex sighs.

It's true – Mum looks amazing.

She's wearing a floaty shirt with a pattern of birds, cut-off denim shorts and flip-flops with jewels on them. My outfit is kind of the same but I'm wearing this cool vest top with a rainbow on it.

"I'm going to have a wedding like this when I'm older!" Bex announces with a grin. She spins around in her party outfit – a T-shirt

dress with a skull and crossbones all in sequins on the front.

I think Mum's plan for her own wedding surprised all the wedding fair stall-holders. But after so many years of making fancy clothes, she wanted something simple for herself. And Danny and the boys were very happy about that. They're all in baggy shorts and Hawaiian shirts.

I spot Danny trying to catch my eye. "OK?" he mouths at me from across the deck.

"Yes!" I mouth back.

I am more than OK. It's funny to think that a year ago, I didn't much like Danny's barge. And I thought I had zero chance of ever getting along with his sons.

But now I can't imagine a time when I didn't know them – the *Bluebell and* the boys!

I gaze around at the dancing party guests, at the twinkling fairy lights, at Danny hugging my laughing mum, at Frank and Tigger zig-zagging through the crowd.

Then I look down at my new little brother and see that Leo is fast asleep on my lap, with one hand around my neck.

Suddenly I realise that I have never been so happy.

There is no camera around to snap me.

But, in the twilight, I smile my brightest ever sunshine smile ...